FLUFFY'S
SCHOOL
ADVENTURES

by **Kate McMullan**

Illustrated by **Mavis Smith**

Scholastic Reader — Level 3

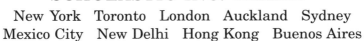

SCHOLASTIC INC.

New York   Toronto   London   Auckland   Sydney
Mexico City   New Delhi   Hong Kong   Buenos Aires

Dedicated to Sharon Zwick
and her first grade class at
Bedford Elementary School

To Maxwell Crook
— K.M.

To Matthew
— M.S.

Fluffy Goes to School (0-590-37213-0)
Text copyright © 1997 by Kate McMullan.
Illustrations copyright © 1997 by Mavis Smith.

Fluffy's 100th Day at School (0-590-52309-0)
Text copyright © 1999 by Kate McMullan.
Illustrations copyright © 1999 by Mavis Smith.

Fluffy's Funny Field Trip (0-439-20673-1)
Text copyright © 2001 by Kate McMullan.
Illustrations copyright © 2001 by Mavis Smith.

Fluffy's Silly Summer (0-590-03269-0)
Text copyright © 1998 by Kate McMullan.
Illustrations copyright © 1998 by Mavis Smith.

Fluffy Meets the Dinosaurs (0-590-52310-4)
Text copyright © 1999 by Kate McMullan.
Illustrations copyright © 1999 by Mavis Smith.

12 11 10 9 8 7 6 5 4 3 2   5 6 7 8 9 10/0

Printed in Singapore   46

This edition created exclusively for Barnes & Noble, Inc.

2005 Barnes & Noble Books

ISBN 0-7607-6772-6

This edition first printing, February 2005

FLUFFY®
GOES TO SCHOOL

by Kate McMullan • Illustrated by Mavis Smith

Hello, Fluffy!

"Close your eyes," said Ms. Day.

"We will pick a name for our new guinea pig."

The guinea pig had his eyes closed.

He was sleeping under some straw.

"How many want Sparky?" asked Ms. Day.
Emma raised her hand.
"How many want Ringo?" asked Ms. Day.
Maxwell raised his hand.
"How many want Fluffy?" asked Ms. Day.
Everybody else raised a hand.

"Open your eyes," said Ms. Day.
"Our guinea pig's name is Fluffy."

"All right!" said Jasmine.
She and Wade slapped hands.

Maxwell walked over
to the guinea pig cage.
"Hello, Fluffy," he said.
The guinea pig opened his eyes.
Fluffy? he thought. **Who is Fluffy?**
Had another animal come into his cage?

The guinea pig looked in his tunnel.

Come out, Fluffy! he growled.

Or I will pull you out!

But no animal came out.

The guinea pig ran over to his food dish.

Get away from my food, Fluffy! he said.

Back away and no one gets hurt.

But no animal was in the food dish.

Two hands picked up the guinea pig.
"Hello, Fluffy!" said Ms. Day.
Fluffy? thought the guinea pig.
Me? You must be joking!

"Hello, Fluffy!" said the whole class.
Fluffy is not a good name for me!
thought the guinea pig. **I'm big and strong!**
"Fluffy is sweet!" said Jasmine.
No way! thought the guinea pig.
I am one bad pig!
"He's so cute!" said Emma.

The hands put Fluffy back in the cage.

I'm out of here, thought the guinea pig.

He went under the straw again.

Soon he was sleeping.

He dreamed that his name was Butch.

Fluffy to the Rescue

Emma and Wade made Fluffy a play yard.
Wade put in a box, a coconut shell,
and a cardboard tube.
Emma put in Fluffy.

Fluffy jumped into the box.
He pretended it was a police car
and he was a policeman.
He chased some robbers.
Stop! called Officer Fluffy.
And I mean now!

"Why are you making so much noise?"
asked Wade.
You are under arrest,
thought Officer Fluffy.

Wade put Fluffy in the coconut shell.

Fluffy pretended it was a boat.

The boat rocked in the storm.

Captain Fluffy held the wheel steady.

The passengers were afraid.

Don't worry, Captain Fluffy told them.

I will save you.

"Stop rocking," Emma said.

"You will get sick."

I never get seasick, thought Captain Fluffy.

Emma picked Fluffy up.
She put him down by the tube.
It looked like a spaceship to Fluffy.

Help! Commander Fluffy!

cried one of the crew.

Space rocks are about to hit the ship!

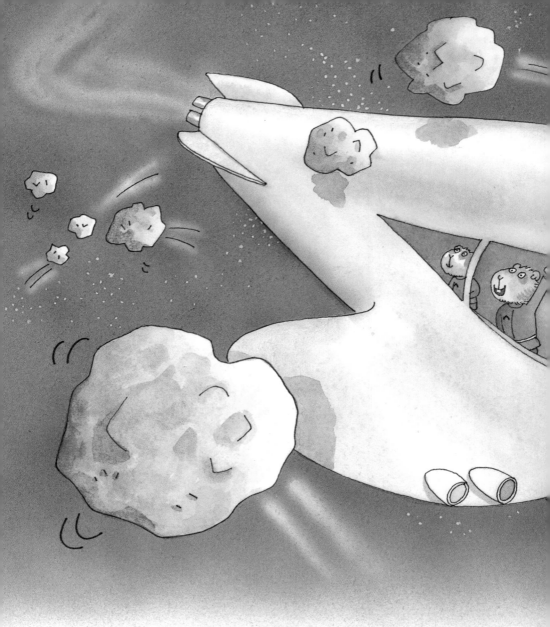

Commander Fluffy sat down.
Put on your seat belts, he said.
This will be a bumpy ride!
Commander Fluffy turned the spaceship
away from a big space rock.

Commander Fluffy turned the spaceship
away from another space rock.
He did it again and again.
Hooray for Commander Fluffy!
shouted the crew.

Now the ship flew into deep space.

But what was this?

Another ship was racing toward them!

Out of the ship came a giant hand!

It turned Commander Fluffy's spaceship
upside down.

Take the ship, crew!

Commander Fluffy called.

I will save you from the giant hand!

"Come out of that tube," said Emma.

Take me to your leader,

thought Commander Fluffy.

Emma put Fluffy back in his cage.
"Have a carrot," said Wade.
Fluffy went to his food dish.
A carrot is good, he thought,
after a hard day at work.

Fluffy the Fast Thinker

Emma took her doll over to Fluffy's cage.

"Fluffy," said Emma, "this is Baby."

Hi, Baby, thought Fluffy.

"Fluffy, would you like to try on Baby's
dress?" asked Jasmine.

No way, thought Fluffy. **Not me!**

Jasmine and Emma put Baby's dress
on Fluffy.

"So pretty!" said Jasmine.

Get me out of here! thought Fluffy.

"Would you like to try on Baby's hat?"
said Jasmine.
No! No! No! No! thought Fluffy.
Emma put Baby's hat on Fluffy's head.
Jasmine tied it under his chin.
"What a little doll!" said Emma.

"Look at baby Fluffy, Ms. Day," said Emma.
"Very cute," said Ms. Day. "But do you think
Fluffy is happy dressed up like that?"
"Sure he is," said Emma.
"He loves it," said Jasmine.
Wrong! thought Fluffy.
Wrong! Wrong! Wrong!

"May we show baby Fluffy
to Ms. Zwick?" asked Emma.
"She was our teacher last year."
"All right," said Ms. Day.
"Just be careful with him."

Jasmine carefully carried Fluffy into
Ms. Zwick's room.
But no one was there.
"Look," said Emma.
"Ms. Zwick's class has a guinea pig, too!"

The girls walked over to see it.
A sign on its cage said DUKE.
"Duke!" Emma called. "Meet Fluffy!"
This can't be happening, thought
Fluffy.

Jasmine put Fluffy down
by Duke's cage.
Duke opened his eyes
and looked at Fluffy.
Who are you?
asked Duke.
WHAT are you?

Fluffy thought fast.

I am a spy, he said.

I am on a secret mission.

That is why I have on these silly clothes.

Wow, said Duke.

"It's time to go, Fluffy," Jasmine said.

"Say good-bye to your new friend."

Duty calls, Fluffy told Duke.

Wow, Duke said again.

Don't tell anyone that you saw me here,
said Fluffy.

I won't say a word, sir, said Duke.

Emma and Jasmine carried Fluffy back to their classroom. They took off the doll clothes and put Fluffy back in his cage. **That was a close one,** thought Fluffy.

FLUFFY'S®
100TH DAY
AT SCHOOL

To my editor, Jordan
—K.M.

To Grace Croteau
—M.S.

FLUFFY'S
100TH DAY
AT SCHOOL

by Kate McMullan • Illustrated by Mavis Smith

Fluffy's Pig Party

It was the 100th day of school.

Ms. Day's class had a party.

After the party, Wade asked,

"Does Fluffy know what day it is?"

"I don't think so," said Ms. Day.

Yes, I do, thought Fluffy.

It is today!

"Let's show Fluffy what 100 means,"
said Jasmine. "Let's have a
'100th day of school' party
for guinea pigs."
And so they did.

Duke came to the party.
So did Kiss.
Lucky Sue came
from the kindergarten.
The kids put all the pigs
into Fluffy's play yard.

Fluffy had never
had a party before.
Uh...hi, he said to the other pigs.
Howdy, said Duke.
I'm a crested pig, said Kiss.
Oh, I just love parties! said Lucky Sue.
Fluffy was not sure
if he liked parties at all.

Emma counted out
100 sunflower seeds.
Maxwell put the 100 seeds
into a bowl in the play yard.
"Party on, pigs!" he said.
The pigs ran over to the bowl.
Wade and Jasmine started counting
how many seeds each pig ate.

Kiss stopped eating.

Let's rock in the coconut shell,

she said.

Oh, I just love to rock!

said Lucky Sue.

What are we waiting for? said Duke.

The pigs ran over to the shell.
Kiss, Duke, and Lucky Sue jumped in.
But there was no room for Fluffy.
He watched the other pigs rock.
He kept eating sunflower seeds.

Yahoo! yelled Lucky Sue. **What fun!**

Fluffy was not having fun.

He ate more sunflower seeds.

Duke started rocking harder.

Lucky Sue rocked like a wild pig.

Kiss rocked so hard that her crest

whipped around on her head.

CRACK! The shell broke.

What a cheap coconut, said Kiss.

I feel like chewing something up,
said Duke.
Oh, I love to chew things up!
said Lucky Sue.
Let's chew up that tube over there,
said Kiss.
No! said Fluffy.
Not my tube!

The pigs ran over to Fluffy's tube.
They started chewing it.
Fluffy nibbled more sunflower seeds
and watched the other pigs chew
his tube to bits.
He did NOT like parties.

"Fluffy just ate the last seed,"
said Jasmine.
She and Wade counted their tally marks.
"Duke ate 10 seeds," Jasmine said.
"Kiss ate 15," said Wade.
"Lucky Sue ate 25.
How many did Fluffy eat?"
"I'm not sure," Jasmine said.
"He ate so fast,
it was hard to count."

Wade added up the seeds
the other pigs had eaten.
"They ate 50 seeds in all," he said.
"Fluffy ate the rest."
"Then Fluffy ate 50 seeds!" said Emma.
"That's half a hundred!"

"The winner of the seed-eating contest
is Fluffy!" said Wade.

"Hooray for Fluffy!" all the kids cheered.

No fair! Kiss told Fluffy.

I didn't know it was a contest!

I didn't know either, said Fluffy.

He burped.

Maybe he liked parties after all.

Fluffy's Big Race

Emma and Jasmine made a race track
100 inches long.
They put the guinea pigs
on the starting line.
I am going to win this race,
said Kiss.
Lucky Sue said, **I love to run!**
Duke smiled. **They don't call me
Speedy Duke for nothing,** he said.
Fluffy burped again.

"On your mark," said Emma.

"Get set. Go!"

The pigs were off!

Duke took the lead.
Kiss and Lucky Sue
were right behind him.
Fluffy tried to catch up.
But he could not go fast.
His tummy was too full
of sunflower seeds.
"Go, Fluffy!" called Emma.

Speedy Duke was really moving.

But then he stopped.

He sniffed.

There were some crumbs on the floor
from the party.

Duke dashed over to the crumbs.

"Duke is out of the race," said Jasmine.

Lucky Sue took the lead.
I love running! she said.
It makes me so happy,
I feel like twirling!
She did a little spin.
Then Lucky Sue
started running again.

"Uh-oh," said Maxwell.
"Lucky Sue is running
the wrong way."
Lucky Sue ran across
the starting line.
I love winning! she said.
"Lucky Sue is out of the race,"
said Maxwell.

Only Fluffy and Kiss were left.
Kiss looked over her shoulder
at Fluffy.
Give up! she told him.
Never! said Fluffy.
He was huffing and puffing.
He promised himself never to eat
50 sunflower seeds again.

Kiss kept looking
over her shoulder.
She was not watching
where she was going.
All of a sudden, she tripped.
Her feet slipped out
from under her.
Ooof! she said as she fell.

"Poor Kiss!" cried Emma.

She quickly picked Kiss up.

Kiss kicked her feet in the air.

Fluffy heard Kiss squealing:

Let go! Put me down!

I have to win this race!

But Emma put Kiss in her lap.

She petted her fur.

"You'll be okay, Kiss," said Emma.

Fluffy kept going all by himself.

At last he crossed the finish line.

"Fluffy ran 100 inches!" said Maxwell.

"Fluffy wins the race!" said Wade.

Fluffy smiled.

They don't call me Fast Fluffy for nothing, he thought.

The Mystery

Ms. Day's kids took
Kiss, Duke, and Lucky Sue
back to their classrooms.
They put Fluffy in his play yard.
Then they went out for recess.
Fluffy's cardboard box
had been turned upside down.
He crawled on top of his box.

He thought about the race,
and how good it felt
to be Fast Fluffy.
A bowl of cherries
was on the counter
next to the play yard.
Big dark red cherries.
They look yummy,
thought Fluffy.
He was starting to feel hungry
again after his big race.

The kids came in from recess.
Ms. Day picked up the bowl.
She said, "Guess how many cherries
Jasmine and Wade put in this bowl?"
"One hundred!" everyone said.
"That's right," said Ms. Day.
"We are going to have them
for a snack. How many people
do we have in this class?"

"There are eighteen kids,"
said Jasmine.
"And one teacher," said Wade.
"That makes nineteen," said Emma.
"And Fluffy makes twenty,"
said Maxwell.
Count me in!
thought Fluffy.

Ms. Day gave Maxwell and Emma
twenty paper cups.
"Please put the cherries
in the cups," she said.
"Each cup will have the same number
of cherries in it."

Emma put one cherry in each cup.

Maxwell put a second cherry in each cup.

Emma put a third cherry in each cup.

Maxwell put a fourth cherry in each cup.

Emma put a fifth cherry in each cup.

But there was no fifth cherry
for the last cup.
"Ms. Day!" Maxwell called.
"The last cup only has four cherries.
There were only 99 cherries
in the bowl."
"We put in 100 cherries," said Jasmine.
"Maybe you counted wrong," said Emma.
"No way," said Wade.
"We counted exactly 100 cherries."
"This is a mystery," said Ms. Day.

Jasmine took the last cup over to Fluffy.
She dumped the four cherries
into his food bowl.
"Four cherries are enough
for you, Fluffy," Jasmine said.
Fluffy jumped off his food box and ran over
to his food bowl.

"Ms. Day!" Jasmine called.
"The mystery is solved."
Everyone ran over
to Fluffy's play yard.
"Look what I found
on top of Fluffy's box," she said.

And she held up a cherry pit.
"My goodness!" said Ms. Day.
"How did Fluffy ever get a cherry?"

Heh heh, thought Fluffy.
**They don't call me Clever Fluffy
for nothing.**

FLUFFY'S
FUNNY FIELD TRIP

FLUFFY'S
FUNNY FIELD TRIP

by Kate McMullan · Illustrated by Mavis Smith

What's For Lunch?

Ms. Day's class
was going on a field trip.
Everyone was rushing around,
getting ready to go.
No one gave Fluffy his lunch.

Emma picked Fluffy up.
"We are going to the planetarium,"
she told him.
"We are going to look at the stars."
Stars, schmars, thought Fluffy.
What's for lunch?

"Line up!" called Ms. Day.
Jasmine ran over to Emma.
"Come on," she said.
"Let's sit together on the bus."
Emma put Fluffy down.
The girls hurried off.

Fluffy sniffed.

Mm-mmm, he thought.

I smell something yummy.

Fluffy followed the yummy smell.

It led to Ms. Day's purse.

Fluffy saw keys.

He saw some money.

He saw a big red apple.

Lunch time! thought Fluffy.

Fluffy dove into the purse.

He took a bite of the apple.

CHOMP!

He took another bite.

Yum, thought Fluffy.

I love lunch!

All of a sudden
the purse started swinging.
Whoa, there! thought Fluffy.
He held onto the apple.

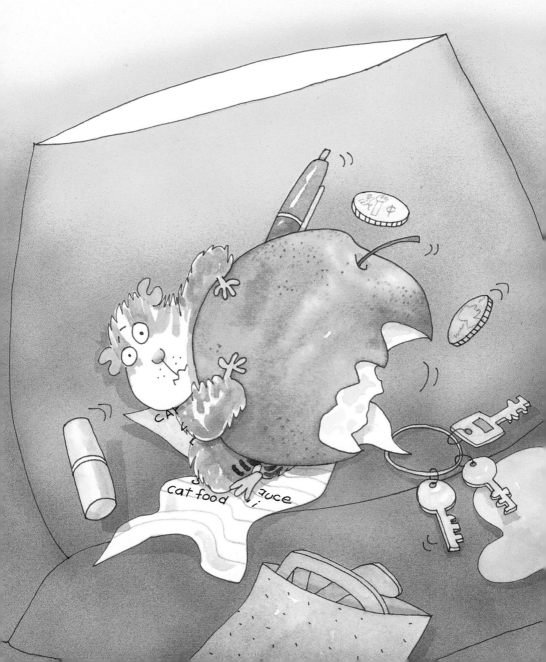

Fluffy rocked this way and that
inside the purse.
His lunch rocked this way and that
inside his tummy.
Ugh! thought Fluffy.
Get me out of here!

At last the swinging stopped.
Fluffy heard an engine start.
Where am I? he wondered.
He heard Ms. Day say,
"You may eat your snacks now."

A hand reached into the purse.
It picked up the apple.
Hey! thought Fluffy.
I'm not finished yet!

"Eew!" said Ms. Day. "My apple!"
Your apple? thought Fluffy.
I don't think so.

Ms. Day picked Fluffy up.
"Fluffy!" she said. "I can't believe
you hid in my purse!"
**I can't believe
you stole my lunch,**
thought Fluffy.

"I'll take care of Fluffy, Ms. Day,"
said Emma.
Ms. Day gave Fluffy to Emma.
She gave her what was left
of the apple, too.

Fluffy quickly finished
the apple.
"Now you can look at the stars
with us, Fluffy," said Emma.
Stars, schmars, thought Fluffy.
What's for dessert?

Fluffy Sees Stars

Ms. Day led her class
into the planetarium.
Everyone sat down.
Emma held Fluffy on her lap.

Slowly, it began to grow dark.

Hey! thought Fluffy.

Who turned out the lights?

A loud voice said,

"Welcome to the night sky!"

Yikes! thought Fluffy.

Who said that?

"What if there were no stars?"
said the voice. "The night sky
would look like this."
Like what? thought Fluffy.
I can't see a thing.

"But the night sky is filled
with stars," said the voice.
Stars popped out
all over the sky.
Everyone said, "Oohhhh!"

"Long ago, people in Greece saw
these same stars," said the voice.
"They thought some groups of stars
looked like pictures. Star pictures
are called constellations."
**All I see are a bunch
of white dots,** thought Fluffy.

"It is not easy to see
star pictures," said the voice.
No kidding, thought Fluffy.
"These lines may help you,"
said the voice.
Lines connecting the stars
appeared in the sky.
"That looks like a giant
connect-the-dots puzzle,"
Emma told Jasmine.

"This is the constellation Pegasus,"
said the voice.

"Pegasus is a horse with wings."
You call THAT a horse?
thought Fluffy.

"The Greeks used long-handled
ladles to dip water," said the voice.
"They called this constellation
the Little Dipper.
That one is the Big Dipper.
Can you see the handle?"

"I see it," said Jasmine.

"Me, too," said Emma.

"Do you see it, Fluffy?"

Oh, sure, thought Fluffy.

But he didn't.

Not really.

"The Big Dipper is part of a bigger
constellation," said the voice.
"It is called Ursa Major,
or the Great Bear."
Where? Where? thought Fluffy.
I can't see any Great Bear.

"The constellations move across
the night sky," said the voice.
Fluffy tried to see the star pictures.
But the dark made him feel sleepy.
Fluffy closed his eyes.
The voice kept talking,
but Fluffy didn't hear a thing.
Zzzzzz, snored Fluffy.

The Great Pig

Welcome to the night sky!

Fluffy told the little guinea pigs.

Look hard!

You can see star pictures!

Where? We can't see anything!
said the little guinea pigs.
Nobody said it was easy,
Fluffy told them. **Maybe
some lines will help.**

**This star picture shows
a flying guinea pig,** said Fluffy.
**We call this constellation
Pigasus.**

Here is the Big Food Bowl.
Next to it is the Giant Carrot,
said Fluffy.
We see them! said the little guinea pigs.

This is the best constellation,
Fluffy told the little guinea pigs.
It is called Fluffy Major,
or the Great Pig.

Is it named after you?
asked the little guinea pigs.
Of course, said Fluffy.

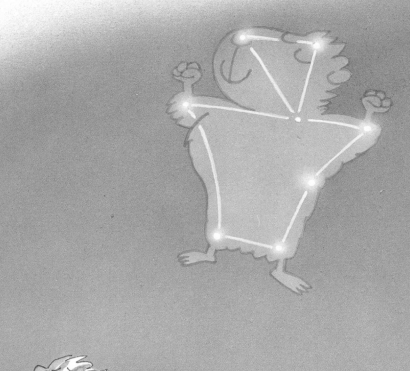

In the sky,
the Great Pig ran over to
the Big Food Bowl.
The Great Bear showed up, too.
Back off! said the Great Pig.
This is my Big Food Bowl.

Grrr! growled the Great Bear.
We could share, said the Great Pig.

The Great Pig ran across the sky.
He picked up the Little Dipper.
He ran back to the Big Food Bowl.
Just one Little Dipper full?
asked the Great Pig.
Grrr! growled the Great Bear.
You win, said the Great Pig.

The Great Pig ran over
to the Giant Carrot.
He was about to take a bite
when Pegasus flew over.
Pigasus flew over, too.

Pegasus took one end of the
Giant Carrot in his teeth.
Pigasus took the other end.
They flew away with it.
Come back! cried the Great Pig.
Come back with my carrot!

"Fluffy?" said Emma.

"Are you having a bad dream?"

Huh? Fluffy woke up.

He was on the bus.

He was on Emma's lap.

"Did you like looking

at the stars?" said Emma.

Stars, schmars, thought Fluffy.
What's for dinner?

FLUFFY'S

SILLY SUMMER

To Super-Tutor Rosemary Hall
— K.M.

To Wills and Georgia
— M.S.

FLUFFY'S
SILLY SUMMER

by Kate McMullan • Illustrated by Mavis Smith

Fluffy the Hero

Fluffy went home with Maxwell
for summer vacation.
Oh, boy! thought Fluffy.
I will nibble grass.
I will lie in the sun.
I love summer!

Maxwell put Fluffy's cage in the den.

He gave Fluffy seeds and water.

"I'm going to the park,"

Maxwell told Fluffy.

"I will see you later!"

Wait! thought Fluffy. **What will *I* do?**

Maxwell's sister, Violet,
came into the den.
"Are you tired of being in that cage?"
she asked Fluffy.
You got that right, thought Fluffy.
"Do you want to go outside with me?"
asked Violet.
Do I ever! thought Fluffy.
Take me to the grass!

Violet picked Fluffy up.

"I'm going to take you swimming,"
she said.

Take me WHAT? thought Fluffy.

Hey! Stop! Wait a second!
thought Fluffy. **I am a land animal!
I walk. I run. I even trot.
But I do NOT swim!**

Violet carried Fluffy outside
to her wading pool.
She put him on the back of a yellow duck.
She pushed the duck
toward the middle of the pool.
"Whee!" she said.

The duck bounced up and down.
Fluffy held onto the duck's neck.
Easy, big fellow, he said to the duck.
I don't want to get wet!

Violet jumped into the wading pool.

"Isn't this fun?" she said.

Not yet, thought Fluffy.

Violet kicked and splashed.

"Whee!" she said.

The duck bounced up and down.

Stop! thought Fluffy. **Whoa, Duckie!**

Then Fluffy saw a fin in the water.
A shark was swimming toward Violet!
Fluffy had to save her!

Go! Go! Go! Fluffy called to his duck.
Fluffy rode toward the shark.
Faster! he called to his duck.

The duck carried Fluffy
over to the shark.
Fluffy hit the shark on the head.
He popped it in the nose.
Fluffy hit him again, right in the teeth!
That did it.
The shark rolled over.

Fluffy the Hero rode his duck
over to Violet.

You are safe now, Violet, thought Fluffy.
That shark will not hurt you.

Violet picked Fluffy up.
No, no, do not thank me,
thought Fluffy the Hero.
I was only doing my job.

Violet dunked Fluffy in the water.
"Whee!" she cried.
A hero's life is never easy,
thought Fluffy.

A Prize for Fluffy

Maxwell, Wade, and Emma
read a sign in a pet shop window.
It said:

BEST PETS CONTEST

Is your pet good-looking?
Is your pet smart?
Can your pet do a trick?
Bring your pet to
Mr. Small's Pet Shop
on Saturday at 1:00.
There will be
PRIZES
for the best pets.

"Fluffy could win a prize," Emma said.

A prize? thought Fluffy.

I'll win ALL the prizes!

On Saturday morning,

Emma washed Fluffy's face and ears.

Maxwell washed Fluffy's paws.

Wade turned him over

and washed his tummy.

Enough! thought Fluffy.

I'm not going for the CLEAN prize!

"We want to enter Fluffy
in the contest," Maxwell told Mr. Small.
You are looking at the big winner!
thought Fluffy.
Mr. Small wrote down Fluffy's name.

All kinds of pets came for the contest.
But there was only one other guinea pig.
Maxwell put Fluffy down beside it.
I am a crested pig,
the other guinea pig told Fluffy.
She scratched her head. **I am
going to win this contest.**

Fluffy's eyes got very big.

The other guinea pig was Kiss!

Kiss did not seem to remember Fluffy.

But Fluffy remembered her.

Kiss had eaten his valentine apple.

Kiss had said his toys were junk.

Fluffy did not like Kiss.

I am beautiful, Kiss told Fluffy.

I am smart. I can do a million tricks.

I will win all the prizes.

I don't think so, said Fluffy.

"Kiss!" called Mr. Small.

A girl took Kiss onto the stage.

Kiss turned around.

Kiss counted to one.

Kiss rolled over.

Fluffy thought Kiss was very good.

He bit his nails.

Can I beat her? he wondered.

Did you see me? Kiss asked
when her turn was over. **I was
really great, wasn't I?**

Kiss scratched her head again.
Fluffy saw some dark spots on her crest.
Kiss had fleas!
One of her fleas jumped onto Fluffy.
Yikes! thought Fluffy.

"Fluffy!" called Mr. Small.

Maxwell carried Fluffy onto the stage.

He put Fluffy down.

Fluffy shook his head.

He shook his arms and his legs.

He had to get that flea off!

Fluffy skipped across the stage.
"Go, Fluffy!" called Wade.

Fluffy turned upside down
and kicked his feet.
"What a pig!" called Emma.

Fluffy scratched his head with one paw.

He rubbed his tummy with the other.

He had to get rid of that flea!

The flea was on Fluffy's head.

All of Fluffy's jumping around had
made the flea very dizzy.

The flea jumped off Fluffy.

Yes! thought Fluffy.

The flea was gone!

He pumped his paw in the air as he
ran off stage.

"Here is a prize," said Mr. Small.
"It is for the best dancer...Fluffy!"
Everyone clapped and clapped.

"Wow," Maxwell said.
"How did Fluffy
get to be such a good dancer?"
I think I will keep that a secret,
thought Fluffy.

Big, Bad Fluffy

Maxwell took Fluffy out to the backyard.
Fluffy looked around.
It's a jungle out here! he thought.
"Keep an eye on Fluffy, Maxwell,"
said his mom.
"Don't worry," said Maxwell.
"Fluffy won't go anywhere."

Maxwell lay down in the backyard.
He put Fluffy down next to him.
Maxwell watched Fluffy nibble grass.
He watched him sniff the ground.
Maxwell closed his eyes.
Fluffy wandered away.

In the jungle, thought Fluffy,
danger is everywhere.

Fluffy walked into the jungle.

A lion poked his head out of the brush.

Get back! thought Fluffy.

**You do NOT want to mess
with a big, bad pig!**

The lion ran back into the brush.

Fluffy made his way through the jungle.
A snake lay in his path.

Go away! thought Fluffy.
Or I will tie you in a big, bad knot!
The snake crawled off.

Fluffy walked deeper into the jungle.
A tiger jumped out at him.

You don't scare me! thought Fluffy.
I'm big! And I'm bad!
The tiger hurried away.

Fluffy smiled.
It is good to be big and bad,
he thought.

Suddenly a dog barked at Fluffy.
Fluffy jumped! He started running.
He saw a hole at the bottom of a tree.
He dove into it to hide.

But the hole was not empty.
It was full of baby rabbits.

Fluffy saw the dog
running for the rabbit hole.
Fluffy jumped into the nest
of baby rabbits.

The dog stuck its head
into the rabbit hole.
Fluffy tried to look
like a cute little bunny.

The dog went away.
Sometimes, thought Fluffy,
it is good to be little and cute.

Just then, Mama Rabbit came home.
Mama Rabbit picked up
one of her babies.
She picked up another one.
She bent down to pick up Fluffy.
Uh oh, thought Fluffy.

You are not one of my babies!
Mama Rabbit said.
She growled at Fluffy.
**Get out of my nest
or you will be sorry!**

Fluffy leaped out of the nest.
He jumped out of the rabbit hole.
He ran across the backyard
straight to Maxwell.

Maxwell opened his eyes.
"I knew you would not go anywhere,"
he said to Fluffy.
Maxwell picked Fluffy up and took him
inside.

Sometimes, thought Fluffy,
it is good to be home.

FLUFFY®
MEETS THE
DINOSAURS

For my fourth-grade friend, Gayle
—K.M.

To "Biff" Heins
—M.S.

FLUFFY
MEETS THE DINOSAURS

by Kate McMullan • Illustrated by Mavis Smith

Fluffy Rules!

Wade and Maxwell put Fluffy
in his play yard.
They put in lots of toy dinosaurs, too.
"Fluffy meets the dinosaurs!" said Wade.
Hey, dinosaurs, thought Fluffy.

"It is the age of the dinosaurs," said Wade.

"Dinosaurs rule the earth."

Those little things? thought Fluffy.

"Dinosaurs are fierce," said Maxwell.

"They are very, very powerful."

You must be joking, thought Fluffy.

Wade picked up a long dinosaur.
He stomped it around.
"I am thunder lizard!" he roared.
In your dreams, thought Fluffy.

Maxwell picked up a big-headed dinosaur.
He stomped it around.
"I am king of the dinosaurs!" he growled.
"T-rex rules!"
I don't think so, thought Fluffy.

Maxwell made T-rex bite Wade's dinosaur.
Wade made his dinosaur roar.
The two dinosaurs began to fight.
Wade and Maxwell made strange
dinosaur noises with their mouths.
Soon more dinosaurs joined the battle.
Hey, watch the food dish! thought Fluffy.
You're messing up my play yard!
But the dinosaurs kept fighting.

"Math time!" called Ms. Day.

Wade and Maxwell put the dinosaurs down.

They went back to their seats.

Fluffy was alone with the dinosaurs.

Fluffy began running around his yard.

He kick-boxed the thunder lizard.

He took a flying leap
and stomped on T-rex.
He kept kicking and stomping.
Soon, not a dinosaur was left standing.

The age of dinosaurs is over,
Fluffy thought.
Now it is the age of guinea pigs.
Fluffy rules!

Fluffy's Great Adventure

"Today is our field trip
to the Natural History Museum,"
Ms. Day told her class.
"Did everyone bring a bag lunch?"
All the kids held up their lunch bags.

Wade put his lunch bag down.

He picked up Fluffy.

"We are going to a dinosaur museum!"

Wade told Fluffy.

Why not a Fluffy museum? thought Fluffy.

"Too bad you can't come," said Wade.

Who says I can't? thought Fluffy.

And when Wade put him down for a second,

Fluffy crawled into Wade's lunch bag.

Ms. Day's class rode a bus to the museum.

Everyone sat in a courtyard to eat lunch.

Wade opened his lunch bag

and took out his sandwich.

"Yuck!" he said.

Fluffy poked his head out of the bag.

Yuck? thought Fluffy. **It was yummy!**

"Yikes!" said Wade when he saw Fluffy.

"Ms. Day!" he called. "Look who's here!"

"Fluffy!" exclaimed Ms. Day.

"How did you ever get into that bag?"

I'll never tell, thought Fluffy.

"Our class pet Fluffy came with us,"
Wade told the museum guide.
The guide took Fluffy from Wade.
"What a pretty little cavy," he said.
Hey, watch your mouth! thought Fluffy.

"*Cavy* is the scientific name
for guinea pig," the guide explained.
"Let's go inside.
I'll show you Fluffy's cousins.
I'll show you his ancestors, which are
his great, great, great, great, great,
great, great, great, great grandparents."

Ms. Day's class followed the guide
into the museum.
They stopped by a glass case.
A sign on the case said RODENTS.
"Rodents are animals that like to gnaw,"
the guide said.
"They have very sharp front teeth.
Fluffy is a member of the rodent family."
Cool, thought Fluffy.

"Mice are rodents, too," the guide said.
"That means mice are Fluffy's cousins."
No way! thought Fluffy.
"So are rats," added the guide.
No, no, no! thought Fluffy.

Fluffy growled.

But the guide did not seem to notice.

He only walked to the next glass case.

"These are Fluffy's ancestors," he said.

"They came from South America.

They are called wild cavies."

Wild! thought Fluffy. **That's me!**

"Wild cavies were plump," the guide said.
"Bigger animals liked to eat them."
Hold it right there! thought Fluffy.

"Only cavies that hid did not get eaten,"
the guide went on. "They survived."
Fluffy looked into the case.
He saw two small furry animals hiding
in the tall grass.
The animals looked very scared.
These are not my ancestors, thought
Fluffy. **No way!**

The guide led the class down the hallway.
He stopped in front of a large statue.

Fluffy's eyes got very big.
Yes! he thought. **Here is my ancestor!**

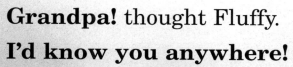

Grandpa! thought Fluffy.
I'd know you anywhere!

T-Fluffy

The guide showed Ms. Day's class
all sorts of dinosaur skeletons.
Some were huge.
Others were as small as lizards.
Some had horns.
Others had wings.
Big deal, thought Fluffy.

"No dinosaurs are alive today,"
the guide said.
"Why not?" asked Wade.
"Some scientists think that
millions of years ago,
a comet hit the earth," the guide said.
"It caused terrible dust storms.
The dust blocked out the sun.

Without sunlight, green plants died.
The dinosaurs had nothing to eat.
So they died, too.
Other scientists think flying dinosaurs
may have changed into birds.
But no one knows for sure."
I do! thought Fluffy. **I do!**

After a comet hit the earth,
tour guide Fluffy told his group,
most dinosaurs died. But not T-rexes.
They were too tough to die.

When dust from the comet
blocked the sun,
the Earth got cold. Brrrr!
It was an ice age.
So what did smart T-rexes do?
They grew fur coats!
Furry T-rexes survived the ice age.

For some reason, guide Fluffy went on,
fur never grew very well on T-rex tails.
So their tails froze and dropped off.
But who needs a tail?

Now, if there was one thing a T-rex loved,
it was a big, juicy carrot.
Luckily, carrots survived the ice age
because they grew underground.
T-rexes got down on all fours
and dug up carrots all day long.
Pretty soon T-rexes forgot that they ever
ran around on their two back legs.
T-rexes became four-legged creatures.

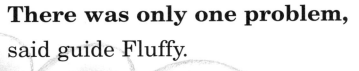

There was only one problem,
said guide Fluffy.
**Big T-rexes had to eat 3 1/2 tons
of carrots every day just to stay alive.**

It was hard work finding so many carrots.

But small T-rexes had it easy. They could fill up on just a few carrots.

So, over millions of years, T-rexes got smaller and smaller.

They ended up no bigger than grapefruits.

And they looked just like...

...me.

Mice and rats are rodents,

said guide Fluffy.

But a guinea pig's ancestors
go back to the age of dinosaurs.

Wade held Fluffy on the bus ride
back to school.
"I wish the dinosaurs were still around,"
he told Maxwell.
"Yeah," said Maxwell. "It would be cool
to have a dinosaur for a class pet."

Yeah, thought T-Fluffy.
Very cool!